EARLY BIRD STORIES™

Fall Pumpkin Fun

Martha E. H. Rustad

Illustrated by Amanda Enright

LERNER PUBLICATIONS ◆ MINNEAPOLIS

NOTE TO EDUCATORS

Find text recall questions at the end of each chapter. Critical-thinking and text feature questions are available on page 23. These help young readers learn to think critically about the topic by using the text, text features, and illustrations.

Lerner Publications Company
A division of Lerner Publishing Group, Inc.
241 First Avenue North
Minneapolis, MN 55401 USA

For reading levels and more information, look up this title at www.lernerbooks.com.

The photos on page 22 are used with the permission of: Mykola Horlov/Shutterstock.com (vine), p. 22; Maleo/Shutterstock.com (colorful pumpkins); Thunderbolt820/Shutterstock.com (orange pumpkins).

Main body text set in Billy Infant 22/28.
Typeface provided by SparkyType.

Library of Congress Cataloging-in-Publication Data

The Cataloging-in-Publication Data for *Fall Pumpkin Fun* is on file at the Library of Congress.
ISBN 978-1-5415-2004-2 (lib. bdg.)
ISBN 978-1-5415-2721-8 (pbk.)
ISBN 978-1-5415-2495-8 (eb pdf)

Manufactured in the United States of America
1-44340-34586-1/24/2018

TABLE OF CONTENTS

CHAPTER 1

PLANTING A PUMPKIN PATCH

It is spring, but I am thinking about fall. Let's grow pumpkins in the garden!

We make little hills in the soil and plant two or three seeds in each hill.

Then we water the seeds.

Later, the seeds crack open.
Tiny roots grow down.

Two weeks pass. **Look!**
I see tiny plants.

Little leaves grow from thin vines.
The vines spread out.

What happens after
the pumpkin seeds
crack open?

CHAPTER 2

FLOWERS AND PUMPKINS

Now it is summer. **Look!**

I see yellow flowers
on the vines.

Buzz! Bees spread pollen from one flower to another.

Little green pumpkins begin to grow. I water the plants every week. They grow bigger all summer.

Leaves take in warm sunlight. Sunlight becomes food for the growing pumpkin plant.

Finally, it is fall.
Cool air and short days tell the pumpkins to stop growing. Their skin turns orange. They are ready to pick!

Why do pumpkins
need sunlight?

15

CHAPTER 3

USING PUMPKINS

Let's make pumpkin pie! First, we wash the pumpkin's skin.

Then we cut up the pumpkin and bake the pieces.

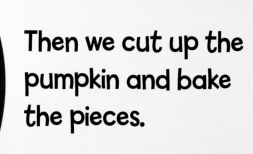

We scoop out the soft flesh and make a pie.

It smells delicious. Yum!

Let's carve a pumpkin. We cut open the top and scoop out the seeds.

We cut out two eyes, a nose, and a mouth.

Don't forget the candle!

Yikes! Our jack-o'-lantern looks spooky.

I save some of the pumpkin seeds. I will plant them next spring.

How big will my pumpkins grow next year?

What can we do with the seeds from a pumpkin?

LEARN ABOUT FALL

Pumpkins need long vines to grow. The vines can grow as long as 30 feet (9 m).

Pumpkins take about one hundred days to grow. The biggest pumpkins can gain up to 25 pounds (11 kg) in a day.

Most pumpkins are orange. But some kinds are blue, white, green, or red. All pumpkins are green when they first begin to grow.

Pumpkins with lots of ridges have a lot of seeds inside of them. Smooth pumpkins have fewer seeds.

The heaviest pumpkin ever weighed 2,625 pounds (1,191 kg). That's about as heavy as a buffalo.

THINK ABOUT FALL:
CRITICAL-THINKING AND TEXT FEATURE QUESTIONS

Why do you think we plant pumpkins in spring instead of fall?

Can you think of any other foods you could make with pumpkin?

How many chapters are in this book?

What is on the back cover of this book?

GLOSSARY

flesh: the soft part of a pumpkin that you can eat

pollen: a tiny yellow dust made by flowers. Flowers need pollen to make seeds.

root: a part of a plant that grows underground. Roots pull up water from the soil.

soil: dirt or earth. Plants grow in soil.

vine: a long stem that grows along the ground

TO LEARN MORE

BOOKS
Deàk, Erzsi. *Pumpkin Time!* Naperville, IL: Sourcebooks Jabberwocky, 2014. Evy is so focused on her pumpkin patch that she doesn't even notice the crazy things happening on her farm, from dancing pigs to flying donkeys.

Lindeen, Mary. *I Pick Fall Pumpkins.* Minneapolis: Lerner Publications, 2017. Learn more about the parts of pumpkins and how they grow.

WEBSITE
Pumpkin Carving
http://www.abcya.com/pumpkin_carving.htm
Play this game and carve your own spooky jack-o'-lantern.

INDEX